This book belongs to:

The Authors

B. Seymour Rabinovitch
Rebecca S. Treger

HiGGLEDY PiGGLEDY

A Tale of Four Little Pigs

CURLY

TWIRLY

WHIRLY

HIGGLEDY PIGGLEDY

Written by **B. Seymour Rabinovitch** *with* **Rebecca S. Treger**
Illustrated by **Mari Gayatri Stein**
Edited by **Ruth A. Rabinovitch**

For more information contact:
Roxy Ann Press, LLC Publisher
ruth.rabinovitch@gmail.com

Library of Congress Control Number: 2013900310

ISBN: 978-0-9887474-0-1

Book Design by Dotti Albertine

Printed in China

This book is dedicated to Human Understanding

The story of Higgledy Piggledy was inspired by the English fairy tale, "The Three Little Pigs", and was told to the four young Rabinovitch children time and time again as they reveled in its happy ending.

What's in a Name?

Growing up in Montreal, Canada in the 1920s—almost a hundred years ago—had its ups and downs. Grade school was not for namby-pambies! Not the last to be teased were children with "funny" surnames—derived mainly from Eastern European parents, newly arrived in the "New World of Opportunity". The name "Rabinovitch" was a heavy load to carry. I often had occasion to wish for a common name, like Smith or Jones, or an easy one, like Berg, Stein, or even Rabin.

But, did you know that name-endings, like "vitch" "wicz", and "ski", simply mean "son of" or "daughter of"? The name of the well known tennis player, Petrova, announces that she is the daughter of Peter, just as Thomson tells us that the bearer is the son of Tom. The Scandinavian ending "sen" tells of a similar relationship: Johannsen—son of John, or Halvorsen—son of a woodsman. And perhaps you have already met with similar meanings in names beginning with "Mac", "Mc", "O'" and "Fitz".

Here, Dear Reader, is a story about a funny-sounding name and what good things may come of it.

HiggLEDY

PiggLEDY

Once upon a time, in the little town of Sudden, there lived four sweet little pigs named CURLY, TWIRLY, WHIRLY, and HIGGLEDY PIGGLEDY. Every day they baked apple pies, played with butterflies in the garden, and took long afternoon naps.

They were as **happy as could be** and never gave a thought to how their world could be an even better place. They certainly never ever thought that one day all might change.

Howevere, one thing put a cloud over Higgledy Piggledy's sunny life. Sometimes, his three brothers made fun of him, teasing, **"Why can't you have a nice easy name?** Our names rhyme like a poem. Your name rhymes like a joke." Curly, Twirly, and Whirly chanted together, "You should have a name like ours. **You should be more like us!"**

As he baked his pies, played in the garden, and settled down to nap, Higgledy Piggledy thought, "I'm happy just the way I am. **Why do they care so much about my name?"** Higgledy Piggledy felt sad. "Maybe it *would* be easier to have a simple name like theirs."

One day, a new neighbor arrived in Sudden and moved in next door to the little pigs. He was a big wolf with pointy teeth and sharp claws. Whenever he saw the four piglets, he would pat his tummy, lick his lips, and think, **"I would love to eat those delicious little pigs!** One pig! Two pig! Three pig! Four!"

"YUM, YUM, YUM, YUM!"

The little pigs saw his teeth and claws and ***they did not trust him!*** Whenever they went out to buy apples for their pies, they made sure that Mr. Wolf was nowhere around. Curly, Twirly, Whirly, and Higgledy Piggledy would open the front door and slowly poke out their heads. First, they would look to the left, then to the right, and then to the left again. After checking to be sure that Mr. Wolf was not in sight, they would pick up their straw baskets and set off.

But **Mr. Wolf was very sly**. As he left his house one morning, he proclaimed loudly, "I have to go away for a while." Then he walked into town, lipperty-lip, licking his lips, and announced to everyone, "I'm on my way out of town." But as soon as he was out of sight, **he sneaked back** and tiptoed around the side of his house to spy on the four little pigs.

That same afternoon, Curly poked his head out of the red front door, looked left and then right and then left again, and saw that Mr. Wolf was not about. **"The coast is clear,"** he said to Whirly, Twirly, and Higgledy Piggledy. "What a perfect time to buy apples." Out they marched in a straight little line, swinging their baskets and singing, *"To market to market to buy our sweet fruit. Then home again home again. Hip-hip toot-toot!* We are such happy little pigs!" they oinked.

Sly Mr. Wolf watched the four piglets leave, and as soon as they had passed his house, **OUT HE SPRANG!** With one swoop of his long, hairy arms he grabbed the four piglets by their tails, took them squealing into his house, and ***locked them in his pantry.***

"Tonight," he said happily, "I'm going to have a delicious feast. I love roast pig and toasted piggy sandwiches." He licked his big lips, ***drooling*** all the while.

The four little pigs were terrified! Curly cried, "Please Mr. Wolf, don't eat us! **We are so good and sweet.**"

Mr. Wolf replied, "Ha! That is precisely why you'll be so delicious!"

Twirly begged, "Please Mr. Wolf, let us go. We are so nice and tidy!"

Mr. Wolf answered with a sneer, "Yes, and I will make neat, **toasted piggy sandwiches** out of you neat pigs."

Whirly cried more sweetly, "Please Mr. Wolf. If you let us go, you can eat us later when we are juicier and plumper."

Mr. Wolf laughed, "Even if you were drier and skinnier, **I'm hungry now.**" Higgledy Piggledy just quivered as he worried about what would happen.

18

Now, Mr. Wolf loved being a winner and thought, "I might have even more fun if we first play a game."

"I've decided that I will give each of you **one chance to be free,"** he announced. "I will let you go, one at a time, and because I'm such a nice wolfie, I'll give you each a head start. As soon as you start running, I'll say your name and then I'll take off and ha, ha! I'll catch you all over again! Who wants to go first?"

"Mr. Wolf!" said brave Curly. "I'll go first."

Mr. Wolf took Curly over to the big front door. He opened it and said, "Remember, **I am going to catch you after I say your name.** Get ready, get set, GO!" Curly took off running on his chubby pink legs as fast as he could.

r. Wolf started counting, "One little piggy, two little piggy, three little piggy, four!" Then he cried out, "Ha, ha, ha! **_Your name is Curly!_**" He bounded after Curly, caught him in a flash, and brought the squealing piglet back to his pantry. Mr. Wolf was very pleased with himself. "I really enjoyed that," he chuckled with a smirk. "Let's play again. **_Who's next?_**"

22

Whirly stepped forward and whispered with a tremor, "I'll g-go."

Mr. Wolf escorted him out of the pantry and said, "You may start running as soon as I open the door. But remember, I'll be after you once I say your name. **_Three, two, one, GO!_**" Whirly started off, huffing and puffing as he ran with all of his heart.

But before he was half-way home, Mr. Wolf shouted, **"Your name is Whirly!"** With his long legs, the wolf set chase and easily caught the poor piglet. Mr. Wolf was very, very pleased with himself as he brought Whirly home to his pantry. **"What fun this is!"** he chortled.

26

"Now who's next?" Mr. Wolf cried.

Plucky Twirly boasted, "I'm the best runner in the family, you'll see."

Mr. Wolf marched him to the front door and said, "Why don't you show me just how fast you are?" As soon as Twirly started running, Mr. Wolf yelled, **"Your name is Twirly."** Quick as a lightning bolt, he raced after the piglet. Before Twirly could get to his doorstep, Mr. Wolf grabbed him around the neck, brought him back to his pantry and dumped him with his brothers. Mr. Wolf was very, very, very pleased with himself!

Finally, it was Higgledy Piggledy's turn. "Okay, Master Young Pig, you're the last of your kin," said Mr. Wolf with an evil smirk. "Here's your chance to best me and save your delicious skin." So, for the fourth time, Mr. Wolf opened the front door and cried, "GO!" As soon as Higgledy Piggledy started running, Mr. Wolf howled, ***"Your name is Piggledy Higgledy."***

"No," Higgledy Piggledy huffed as he ran for his life. "That's wrong!"

"Oh," screeched Mr. Wolf. "Now I've got it, it's ***Wiggledy Piggledy.***"

"Wrong again," puffed Higgledy Piggledy as he lengthened his lead.

"Higgledy Wiggledy?...Wiggledy Diggledy?... I've finally got it— ***Higgledy Piggledy!***" Mr. Wolf cheered and bolted after the piglet.

ut Higgledy Piggledy was just at his own door. He opened it quickly and slammed it shut on Mr. Wolf's nose. Through the door, Higgledy Piggledy shouted, "I beat you, Mr. Wolf."

Mr. Wolf growled, "Oh fiddle sticks, I've lost him! No matter, **I've got three other young piglets to eat**, and that's still a feast." He trudged back home, started a fire, and began laying the table for dinner.

"**H**oly old bald head!" Mr. Wolf suddenly exclaimed, clapping his paw to his forehead. "I've run out of bread. I'll have to buy another loaf. After all, I can't make toasted piggy sandwiches without any bread." He put on his hat and started off to the market.

Little did the wolf know, Higgledy Piggledy was peering out from behind his curtains. As soon as Mr. Wolf was out of sight, Higgledy Piggledy hurried over to Mr. Wolf's house and rushed inside to unlock the pantry. "Come on, come on!" he shouted to Curly, Whirly and Twirly. ***"Let's get away before Mr. Wolf returns!*** Quickly, you three! Hurry!" The little pigs ran straight home and locked themselves behind their big red door, safe at last.

Soon, Mr. Wolf returned home. **"*Oh yum, yum! Dinner will be fun,*"** he sang as he unlocked the pantry and waltzed inside. But, lo and behold, no piglets! With a befuddled stare, Mr. Wolf blinked twice and could not believe his eyes!

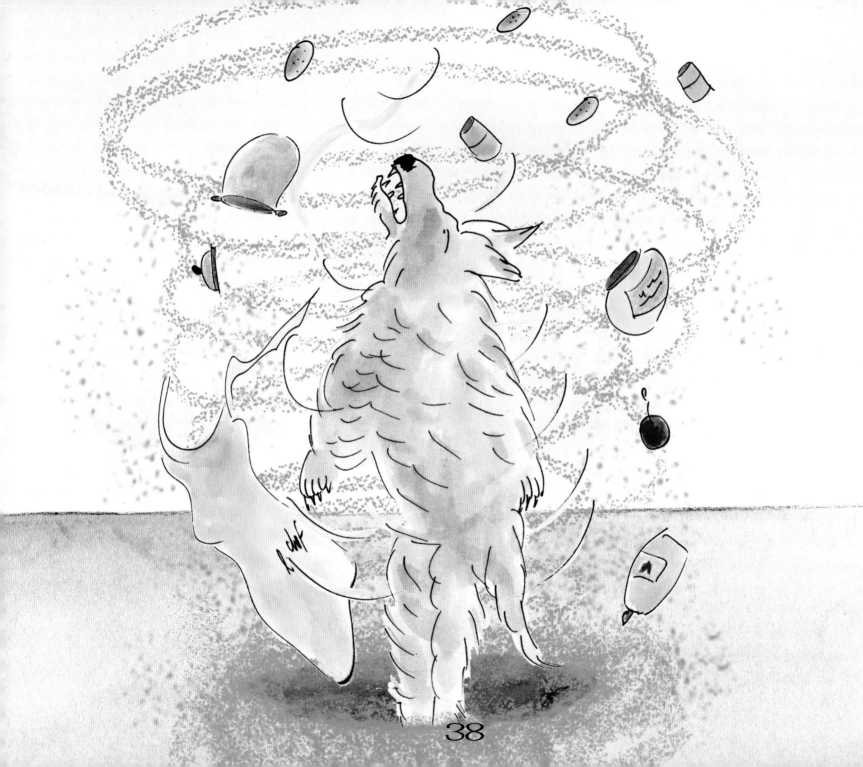

Mr. Wolf realized that he had been outsmarted by little Higgledy Piggledy. He was so furious that he started spinning around and around, faster and faster, boring a hole right through the floor. Finally, in a cloud of sawdust and dirt, he drilled straight down and disappeared from sight. Some say that he ended up in China on the other side of the world. The only thing the sweet piglets knew was that **Mr. Wolf was never seen again.**

Safely back home, Curly, Whirly, and Twirly knew that Higgledy Piggledy, with his long, awkward name that didn't rhyme with anything, had saved their lives.

"You are the bravest and smartest of us all," said Curly. **"We shouldn't have made fun of you,"** added Twirly.

"Please forgive us—we are so sorry!" oinked Whirly.

Higgledy Piggledy did forgive them and the four little pigs returned to their normal lives, baking apple pies, playing in the garden, and taking long naps. And sometimes, Curly, Twirly, and Whirly would look at their brother and wish that they, too, had a name that could have saved the day.

About the Authors

DR. B. SEYMOUR RABINOVITCH, a retired professor of chemistry, enjoyed a long academic career at the University of Washington, in Seattle. The youngest of seven children, he was raised and educated in Montreal, Canada. During World War II, he served in Europe as an officer in the Canadian Army. In retirement, he has found continuing pleasure in writing children's tales and rhymes. He may be reached at Department of Chemistry, Box 351700, University of Washington, Seattle, WA 98195-1700.

REBECCA SIMONE TREGER, Dr. Rabinovitch's granddaughter, was raised in Medford, Oregon and has a lifelong love of reading, folktales and storytelling. Rebecca loves tap dancing, cooking, and travel and is pursuing a career in medical research.

About the Illustrator

MARI GAYATRI STEIN is an author, artist and cartoonist whose insightful words and drawings have delighted readers. She has written and illustrated ten books, including *Puddle Moon, Unleashing Your Inner Dog,* and *The Buddha Smiles.* Mari has taught yoga and meditation for three decades and lives with her husband in southern Oregon.